May Magic

"You turned our mom into a duck!" Brian yelled.

Bradley couldn't open his mouth. He just stared at the duck. It stood in the middle of the stage and looked at the audience. Then it sat down and began preening its feathers. The bracelet around the duck's neck glistened under the lights.

"My goodness!" said Hypo. "I guess I used too much magic!"

Hypo got down on one knee next to the duck. "Pamela, can you hear me?" he said into the duck's ear.

The duck said, "Quack!"

The audience was totally quiet. You could have heard a feather drop.

Hypo turned to the audience. "What should we do?" he asked.

"Change her back!" Bradley and Brian yelled together.

Calendar Mysteries

May Magic

HYPO the HYPNOTIST
is coming to Green Lawn
ONE NIGHT ONLY!

by Ron Roy

illustrated by
John Steven Gurney

A STEPPING STONE BOOK™

Random House New York

This is dedicated to my pal, Darlene Zoller:
dancer, friend, inspiration.
—R.R.

To Maxi
—J.S.G.

Text copyright © 2011 by Ron Roy
Cover art and interior illustrations copyright © 2011 by John Steven Gurney

Visit us on the Web!
ronroy.com
www.randomhouse.com/kids

Educators and librarians, for a variety of teaching tools, visit us at
www.randomhouse.com/teachers

Library of Congress Cataloging-in-Publication Data
Roy, Ron.
May magic / by Ron Roy ; illustrated by John Steven Gurney.
    p.   cm. — (Calendar mysteries)
"A Stepping Stone book."
Summary: Bradley and Brian need help from Nate and Lucy after a hypnotist
turns their mother into a duck but does not quite get her changed back.
ISBN 978-0-375-86111-6 (trade) — ISBN 978-0-375-96111-3 (lib. bdg.) —
ISBN 978-0-375-89832-7 (ebook)
[1. Mystery and detective stories. 2. Hypnotism—Fiction. 3. Ducks—Fiction. 4. Practical
jokes—Fiction. 5. Twins—Fiction. 6. Brothers and sisters—Fiction. 7. Cousins—Fiction.]
I. Gurney, John Steven, ill. II. Title.
PZ7.R8139Maw 2011
[Fic]—dc22
2010001375

Printed in the United States of America

10 9 8 7 6 5 4 3 2 1

Contents

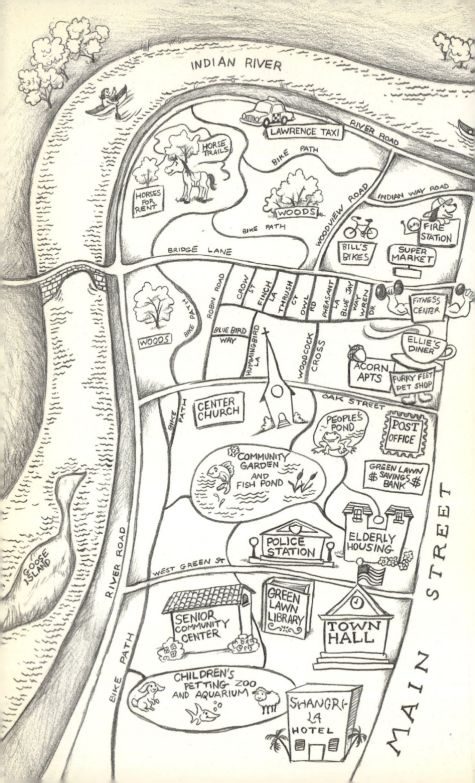

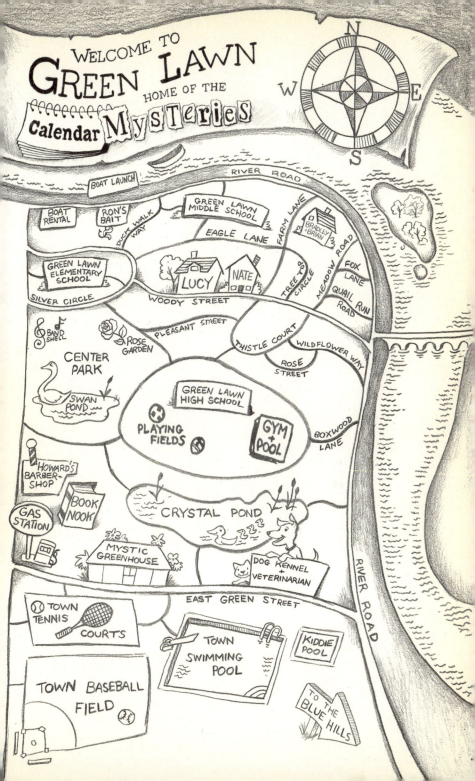

1
Brian's Great Idea

"No, she won't!" Bradley said. He and his twin brother were in their room. They were lying on their beds, reading comics. Bradley was wearing his I'M BRADLEY T-shirt. The family dog, Pal, was chewing on a tennis ball.

"Yes, she will!" Brian said. His bed was covered with toys, clothing, games, sneakers, books, and a damp bath towel. His T-shirt said, I'M BRIAN.

"Bet she won't," Bradley said. His bed was neat.

"Bet she will," Brian said.

Their mother knocked and walked into the room. "Bet I will what?" she asked Brian.

"Brian wants to raise ducks," Bradley said. "I told him you'd say no."

Mrs. Pinto looked at Brian. "Your bed is a mess," she said. She picked up the bath towel. "And why do you want to raise ducks?"

Brian held up a page in his comic book. "Look at this, Mom. Ducks can make me rich!"

His mother read the page. In big letters an ad said: RAISE DUCKS AND MAKE BIG BUCKS!!!

"Darling, running a business is hard work," Brian's mother said. "Besides, I can't even get you to clean your side of the room!"

"If I clean my room, can I have ducks?" Brian asked.

"No, dear, you're only six years old," his mother said. "Besides, you already have a dog and a pony to play with."

"I don't want to play with ducks," Brian answered. He held up the comic again. "It says here you can collect their feathers and make pillows. Then you sell the pillows and make a lot of money!"

"Do you know how to make pillows?" Brian's mother asked.

Bradley giggled.

"Cinchy," Brian said. "You just sew some cloth and stuff it with feathers!"

His mother smiled. "Honey, you don't know how to sew."

Bradley cracked up. "Told you so," he said. "Get it? SO!"

"Okay, you two, please get this room cleaned up," their mother said. "Tomorrow is Mother's Day, and I want this house spotless!"

"But my side is already spotless," Bradley said.

"So help your brother clean his side," his mother said as she left the bedroom with the towel. She stopped and turned around. "If you do a good job, I'll give you each one dollar."

Bradley put his comics neatly on his shelf. "Get busy, Brian," he said.

"I like my side of the room messy," he said.

"Yeah, but Mom doesn't, and she's boss," Bradley said.

"Why can't we have a mom who lets us be slobs?" Brian asked. He kicked some of the junk off his bed. "Mother ducks don't make their baby ducks clean their rooms."

Bradley laughed. "Baby ducks don't have rooms," he said. "They have ponds."

Brian smiled. "Let's build a pond in

our room," he said. "Then we can sneak in some ducks!"

"Are you kidding?" Bradley asked. "Mom would have a cow!"

"I don't want a cow," Brian said. He sighed and began tossing his junk into a closet. "Are you gonna help me?"

"Sure," Bradley said. He began sorting Brian's comics and games and toys. "What's this?" He held up a sheet of paper.

"It came in the mail with one of my comics," Brian said.

Bradley read the sheet. "Hey, Bri, look at this."

Bradley showed his brother a picture of a man with a top hat and mustache. Under the picture it said: HYPO THE HYPNOTIST IS COMING TO GREEN LAWN! ONE NIGHT ONLY!!!

"He's coming here?" Brian asked. "When?"

"He's doing a show at the high school tonight," Bradley said. "I wonder if Mom and Dad will let us go."

Brian dropped a sneaker. "I've got a better idea!" he shouted. "We'll take Mom to the show and ask the guy to hypnotize her! While she's in a trance, Hypo will tell her she loves ducks!"

Bradley shook his head. "First, Mom would never go. She thinks hypnotists are all fake," he said. "Second, I heard that hypnotism doesn't work if the person doesn't want to be hypnotized. And Mom would never let some guy put her in a trance!"

Just then Josh walked into their room. "This place is disgusting," he said. He kicked a foam ball out of his way.

"We're cleaning it," Bradley said.

"You'd better," Josh said. "Mom wants the house looking good for Mother's Day tomorrow. I bought Mom

her favorite nail polish. What'd you guys get her?"

Brian flopped on his bed. "We have to buy a gift?" he asked.

"Duh!" Josh said. "It is Mother's Day, bro! Dad bought her a nice bracelet."

Bradley picked up his piggy bank and shook it. "I've got a bunch of money!" he announced. "What should we get her, Brian?"

Brian grinned. "Baby ducks?"

"I know what she wants," Josh said.

"Tell us!" Bradley shouted.

"She wants to go see Hypo the Hypnotist at the high school tonight," Josh said.

"She does?" Bradley asked. "I thought she hated those guys!"

Josh shrugged. "All I know is what she told me," he said. "She wants to see Hypo, and she wants to wear her new bracelet and nail polish." He kicked a soccer ball on his way out of the room.

An evil look came over Brian's face. "Mom wants to go see Hypo? This is gonna be perfect," he whispered.

2
The World's
Greatest Hypnotist

"This is so exciting," Bradley and Brian's mother said. "Thank you boys for taking me!"

"But, Mom," Bradley said, "you always told us hypnotists were all phonies."

His mother pointed to a giant poster of Hypo in front of the high school. "Hypo isn't," she said. "He's world-famous!"

"Come on," Brian said. "Let's get some good seats."

The high school auditorium was crowded and noisy. Bradley and Brian were joined by their best friends, Nate and Lucy. Josh went to sit with Lucy's cousin Dink and Nate's sister, Ruth Rose.

"Mrs. Pinto, I love your bracelet!" Lucy said.

"Thank you, sweetie," Mrs. Pinto said. "Mr. Pinto gave it to me for Mother's Day." She wiggled her fingers. "And Josh gave me this pink nail polish!"

"We bought her tickets to see Hypo!" Brian said.

"I bought the tickets," Bradley said. "Brian is broke!"

A few minutes later the lights in the auditorium dimmed. The crowd became quiet. A round man with a bald head stepped in front of the curtain. He raised his arms and smiled.

"That's Mr. Creakey, the high school

principal," Bradley's mother whispered.

A lot of people clapped. Someone yelled, "Hi, Mr. C. Gonna get hypnotized?"

A boy hurried onto the stage and handed Mr. Creakey a microphone.

"Good evening, all!" Mr. Creakey bellowed into the mike. His voice made a loud screechy noise all over the auditorium.

Mr. Creakey held the mike farther from his mouth. "Sorry about that," he said. "No, I won't be hypnotized tonight. But some of you will! Now, without further delay, it is my pleasure to introduce Hypo, the world's greatest hypnotist!"

Mr. Creakey hurried off the stage just as the curtain behind him opened. The stage lights went out. The audience was staring at a completely black stage.

"I can't see anything!" Nate whispered. "This is spooky!"

Suddenly a spotlight flashed on, making a circle on the stage. Inside the circle stood Hypo, wearing a tuxedo and top hat and holding a wand. A black mustache covered his upper lip. He bowed, and the audience began clapping and cheering. Then the rest of the stage was lit.

Hypo was standing between a sofa and a tall booth. The booth was painted bright red, with a gold curtain across its front. A water pitcher and glasses stood on a small table next to the booth.

"Good evening, one and all!" said Hypo. His voice was deep and smooth. It flowed over the audience like melted chocolate.

"I love being back in Green Lawn. I attended this high school," the hypnotist said. "Yes, I graduated seventeen years ago. I used to work in the Shangri-la Hotel on weekends. I'd stop at Ellie's

Diner for ice cream on my way to work."

"Mom, did you know that?" Bradley whispered.

She nodded and smiled.

Hypo stepped closer to the audience. He grinned. "Now, who would like to be hypnotized this evening?" he asked.

Bradley could hear some laughter coming from the front row. Then a teenager stood up. His friends shoved him toward the stage.

"Don't be shy!" Hypo said. "Hypo won't hurt you!"

The kid stumbled up the stairs and stood next to Hypo on the stage. Everyone clapped and whistled.

"What is your name, young man?" Hypo asked the nervous boy.

"Ch-Chad," the boy stuttered.

"Hello, Chad," Hypo said. "Why do you want me to hypnotize you?"

Chad grinned. "My friends dared me," he said. "I didn't want to be a chicken."

Hypo stared at Chad. Then he turned to the audience. "Shall I turn Chad into a chicken?" he asked. "Make him cluck and eat bugs?"

"No!" someone yelled. "Make him disappear!"

Everyone laughed.

Chad held up his hands. "Can you make me stop biting my nails?" he asked.

"Goodness, Chad," Hypo said. "Don't your parents feed you? You've chewed those nails entirely off your fingers!"

"Bad Chad!" one of his buddies yelled.

Hypo pointed to the sofa with his wand. "Please be seated, Chad."

The boy sat.

"Now look into my eyes, Chad."

Chad stared into Hypo's eyes.

The audience was silent.

Hypo slowly passed his wand before Chad's eyes. Back and forth went the wand.

"Close your eyes, Chad," Hypo said in a soft voice.

Chad closed his eyes.

The audience remained silent as Hypo spoke:

> CHAD DOESN'T WANT TO
> CHEW HIS NAILS.
> HYPO HELPS WHEN ALL
> ELSE FAILS.
> SOON THIS BOY WILL BE
> STRONGER.
> THEN HIS NAILS WILL
> GROW LONGER.

"When you open your eyes, your problem will be solved!" Hypo said. "You will never chew your nails again! Open your eyes, Chad!"

Chad opened his eyes. He blinked and grinned.

"Now, Chad, I want you to bite your nails," Hypo said. "Do it, Chad! Chew those fingernails! Yum yum, fingernails are delicious!"

Chad moved one hand toward his mouth. Then he stopped. "I can't do it!" he said.

Hypo pulled a wallet from his pocket. "Chad, I will give you twenty dollars if you chew your nails!"

Again Chad tried, but he could not chew his nails. He grinned at Hypo. "You're good, dude," he said.

Hypo turned to the audience. "Chad is cured!" he cried.

The audience cheered as Chad left the stage to join his friends.

"That was so cool!" Brian said. He nudged Bradley. "Hey, Mom, why don't you get hypnotized?"

3
Mom Is Ducky

"Don't be silly," Brian's mom said to him. "Why would I want to let Hypo hypnotize me?"

Just then Hypo walked to the edge of the stage. He shaded his eyes so he could see into the audience. "Are there any other volunteers?" he asked.

Brian jumped to his feet. "Yeah, my mom!" he said.

Bradley pulled his brother back into his seat. "What are you doing?" he whispered.

"You'll see," Brian said. "We're over here, Mr. Hypo!"

Hypo walked down the stage stairs. He marched to the row where Bradley was sitting with his mother and brother. Nate and Lucy turned around in their seats and stared at Brian.

"Are you gonna do it, Mrs. Pinto?" Nate asked.

Before Bradley's mother could answer, Hypo was standing next to her. He put out his hand. "Hello, I'm Hypo. What is your name?"

Bradley's mother shook Hypo's hand. "I'm Pamela Pinto," she said. "But I'm not interes—"

"Pamela Pinto, what a lovely name," said Hypo. "Won't you join me on the stage? Your handsome twins can come with you."

"Gee, Bradley, we're handsome!" Brian crowed.

"Well, I don't know," their mother said.

"Do it, Mom!" Brian said.

"Go for it, Mrs. Pinto," Nate said.

"It'll be fun!" Lucy said.

Only Bradley remained quiet. He knew that Brian had a plan. Bradley wondered if Hypo could really hypnotize his mom so she'd let Brian raise ducks!

"Okay, come on, boys," Mrs. Pinto said. She followed Hypo back to the stage. Bradley and Brian were right behind her.

The whole audience clapped and whistled.

Hypo sat the twins' mother on the sofa, with Bradley and Brian next to her.

"Pamela Pinto, do you chew your nails?" Hypo asked.

"Of course not!" she said. She held up her hands.

"What lovely pink nail polish," Hypo said.

"Yes, my son Josh gave it to me for Mother's Day," she said. "And my husband gave me this bracelet."

"And what did these two young men give you for Mother's Day?" Hypo asked. He pointed his wand at Bradley and Brian.

"They bought the tickets to see your show," she said.

"Such nice sons you have!" Hypo said. "So, boys, what shall we do with your mother?" he asked.

Bradley didn't know what to say.

But Brian did. "My mom doesn't like ducks," he said. "Can you hypnotize her so she loves them?"

Brian's mother glared at him. "I never said I didn't like du—"

"That's an excellent idea!" Hypo said. "What do you folks think?"

The audience cheered and clapped.

"Okay, Mrs. Pinto, please close your eyes," Hypo said.

She closed her eyes. "I feel silly," she said.

Brian giggled, and Bradley poked him in the ribs.

Hypo passed his wand over Mrs. Pinto's head. He muttered some strange words.

"Mrs. Pinto, please open your eyes," Hypo said after a minute.

She opened her eyes.

"Mrs. Pinto, do you like animals?" Hypo asked.

"Of course I do," she said. "We own a dog and a pony, and I had rabbits when I was a girl."

"Marvelous. Now tell our audience your favorite animal."

"Well, I'll have to think a moment," Mrs. Pinto said.

"Take your time," Hypo said. He gave the audience a big wink.

"I'd have to say songbirds," Mrs. Pinto said finally. "We have several bird feeders in our yard."

"Excellent, you are fond of our flying friends," Hypo said. He leaned toward her. "Now, Pamela, tell us how you feel about ducks."

"I don't like them," she said. "Ducks are noisy and messy and they would destroy my garden!"

The audience laughed.

Bradley laughed.

Brian didn't laugh.

Hypo didn't laugh, either. He scratched his chin. "Hypo will have to try something else," he said. "Mrs. Pinto, will you please come with me?"

He walked her over to the red booth. He swept the curtain aside. "Will you step inside, please?"

The twins' mother stepped into the booth. Hypo closed the curtain.

He turned toward the audience. "I must have absolute silence!" he said.

The auditorium went quiet.

On the sofa, Bradley listened to his own heartbeat.

Hypo closed his eyes and spoke:

PAMELA PINTO LOVES
THE BIRDS.
PAMELA PINTO HEARS
MY WORDS.
WITH SUPER MAGICAL
HYPO LUCK,
MAKE PAMELA PINTO
LOVE A DUCK.

Then he yanked the gold curtain aside.

Bradley's mother was gone!

In her place stood a big white duck.

The audience went wild.

Bradley thought he would keel over.

The duck waddled out of the booth. Even from the sofa, Bradley could see that the duck had pink nail polish on its toenails.

Hanging around the duck's neck was his mom's new bracelet.

4
Too Much Magic

"You turned our mom into a duck!" Brian yelled.

Bradley couldn't open his mouth. He just stared at the duck. It stood in the middle of the stage and looked at the audience. Then it sat down and began preening its feathers. The bracelet around the duck's neck glistened under the lights.

"My goodness!" said Hypo. "I guess I used too much magic!"

Hypo got down on one knee next to

the duck. "Pamela, can you hear me?" he said into the duck's ear.

The duck said, "Quack!"

The audience was totally quiet. You could have heard a feather drop.

Hypo turned to the audience. "What should we do?" he asked.

"Change her back!" Bradley and Brian yelled together.

"CHANGE HER BACK!" the audience chanted. "CHANGE HER BACK, CHANGE HER BACK!"

"Very well," Hypo said. "But we must have silence. You're scaring the duck . . . I mean you're scaring Mrs. Pinto."

The audience settled down again.

Hypo shooed the duck back into the booth and closed the curtain.

Then he closed his eyes and spoke:

PAMELA DOESN'T WANT
TO QUACK.

HYPO WILL NOW CHANGE
HER BACK.
WITH MY MAGIC AND
HYPO LUCK,
SHE'LL NO LONGER BE
A DUCK!

Hypo swept the curtain open and
Mrs. Pinto stepped out.

The audience broke into cheers and
whistles.

"Mom!" Bradley cried. He jumped up
and hugged his mother.

"How do you feel, Pamela?" Hypo
asked.

"Thirsty," she said. "Do you suppose
I could have a glass of water? I'm feeling
extremely thirsty!"

Hypo poured Mrs. Pinto a tall glass
of water. She drank it down and held out
the empty glass.

"Thank you," she said. "May I have

another? I don't know why I'm so thirsty. I just crave water!"

Hypo gave Mrs. Pinto a second glass of water. She gulped it down and handed him the glass.

"Pamela, may I ask how you feel about ducks now?" Hypo asked. "Do you still dislike them?"

"What a silly question," Mrs. Pinto said. "I adore ducks. I love the way they waddle and splash in the water!"

Brian poked his brother. "See, Bradley? Mom adores ducks," he whispered. "It worked!"

Bradley couldn't believe his eyes and ears.

Hypo beamed at the audience. "Thank you, Pamela Pinto. Thank you, boys!" he said.

The audience cheered as Bradley followed Brian and their mom off the stage. Bradley noticed a white feather stuck to the hem of her dress.

Back in their seats, Bradley snuck a look at his mother. Did she really love ducks now? he wondered. Would she let Brian raise them? Shaking his head, Bradley sat back to watch the rest of the show.

"Boy, Mom's been in the bathroom a long time," Brian said the next morning.

"I know," Bradley said. He was sitting on his bed, waiting to brush his teeth. "Did you knock on the door?"

Brian threw himself on his bed. "Yup. She's taking a bath—a long bath. I can hear her splashing around in there."

"Weird," Bradley said. "When we splash in the tub, she yells at us."

"Yeah, no fair," Brian said. "Plus, she always took showers before. Anyway, when she comes out, I'm going to ask her."

"Ask her what?" Bradley asked.

"If I can get some ducks to raise," Brian said. He grinned at his brother. He had an evil twinkle in his eye. "Now that she loves ducks so much, she's bound to let me. Thanks to Hypo!"

"Do you really think she got hypnotized last night?" Bradley asked. "Hypo looks like a big phony to me."

"Duh, he turned Mom into a duck!" Brian said. "Then he turned her back. What's phony about that?"

Bradley sat on his bed and thought about what had happened at the high school last night. "Did you notice anything strange about Mom when we got home?" he asked.

"Like what?" Brian asked.

"Well, she didn't yell when we ate ice cream before bed," Bradley said. "She NEVER lets us eat before bedtime."

Brian stared at his twin brother.

"You're right!" he said. "And she didn't even remind us to brush our teeth."

Bradley looked at the clock. It was almost ten-thirty. "And she didn't tell us to make our beds this morning. It's almost like she doesn't care what we do."

"Cool!" Brian said. He picked up a comic book. Bradley tiptoed into the hallway and stood outside the bathroom door. He could hear splashing and his mom singing. He put his ear against the door.

Bradley tore back into his room. "Brian, you have to hear this. Come on!"

The boys huddled next to the bath-room door with their ears against the wood. They heard their mother singing:

SIX LITTLE DUCKS
THAT I ONCE KNEW—
SHORT ONES, FAT ONES,

SKINNY ONES, TOO.
BUT THE ONE LITTLE DUCK
WITH THE FEATHER ON HIS
    BACK,
HE RULED THE OTHERS
WITH HIS QUACK, QUACK,
    QUACK!

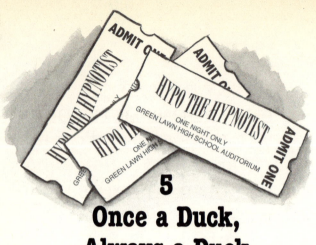

5
Once a Duck,
Always a Duck

"Brian, she's quacking and singing duck songs! Mom's still a duck!" Bradley gasped.

They raced back to their room. "Hypo must've messed up again!" Bradley said. "She looks like Mom, but she's a duck!" He threw himself on his bed.

Brian laughed. "Good thing I didn't ask Hypo to make her love rhinos!" he said.

Just then Josh walked into the twins'

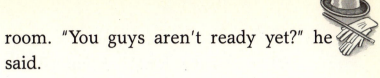

room. "You guys aren't ready yet?" he said.

"Ready for what?" Brian asked.

"Dude, it's Mother's Day," Josh said. "Dad's taking us all out for lunch. You guys have to take showers and wear clean clothes."

"We would except we can't get in the bathroom," Brian said. "Mom's been in there for hours!"

"Yeah, she's playing in the tub like a kid," Bradley added. *Or like a duck,* he said to himself.

"Have you noticed anything different about Mom?" Brian asked Josh.

Josh thought for a minute. "Not really," he said. "But . . ."

"But what?" Bradley asked.

"Last night after we got home from the high school, I came down for a snack," Josh said. "Mom was in the kitchen."

"What was she doing?" Brian asked.

"Well, she had all these vegetables on the table," Josh said. He had started to whisper. "There was corn, peas, lettuce, a whole bunch of stuff. And she was eating it all, but she wasn't using a knife and fork."

The twins just stared at Josh.

"Guys, she was eating with her fingers!" Josh said. "And for the peas, she didn't even use her fingers!"

"You mean she just . . . ," Bradley said.

"Yup. She just bent over and ate them off the table, like Pal does with his treats."

Or like a duck eats, Bradley thought. He glanced at Brian. By the look on Brian's face, Bradley knew his twin was thinking the same thing. Their mom was a duck!

The three brothers jumped when

their mother suddenly appeared in the bedroom. She was wearing a fluffy white bathrobe. "The bathroom's all yours, boys," she said. Then she hurried down the hall.

"Be ready in a half hour," Josh said to the twins, then went to his own room.

"What are we gonna do?" Bradley asked.

"About what?" Brian asked.

"Our mother, you dope!" Bradley said. "She's eating like a duck. She's quacking and singing duck songs and splashing in the tub. Next thing you know, she'll be flying around the house! You and your brilliant idea to have her hypnotized!"

"Chill out," Brian said. "So what if she eats with her fingers. She's still our mom."

"SHE'S A DUCK!" Bradley yelled. "And what's Dad going to say when he finds out he's married to a bird?"

"Dibs on the shower!" Brian yelled. He grabbed his towel and ran for the bathroom.

Bradley didn't care if his brother got the shower first. He was getting a headache. He should never have let Brian talk their mom into going up on the stage with Hypo.

Bradley followed Brian down the hallway. Suddenly he heard a scream from the bathroom. Brian stuck his head out the door. "Bradley, come here, quick!"

Bradley walked into the bathroom. His bare feet crunched on something. He looked down. He was walking on corn kernels, the kind you use to make popcorn. The stuff was all over the floor.

Brian grabbed Bradley and pulled him over to the tub. He yanked the shower curtain back.

Bradley gasped. Piled on the bottom of the tub were at least ten yellow rubber duckies.

6
Mud Puddles for Mom

"Where did they come from?" Brian asked.

"We used to play with them in the tub when we were little," Bradley said. "I think Mom kept them up in the attic."

Brian stared at his brother. "You think she really is a . . ."

"Yes, I do," Bradley said. "And it's your fault!"

"What did I do?" Brian asked.

"Oh, nothing, only getting Mom hypnotized," Bradley said.

"But then she got *un*-hypnotized!" Brian argued. "Can I help it if Hypo messed up?"

Josh poked his head into the bathroom. "Showers, you guys," he said. "I want this bathroom in ten minutes. And leave it clean!"

A half hour later the family was in the car heading for town. Their dad was taking them to a restaurant called Lily's Pad. It was on the Indian River at the end of Oak Street.

The three boys were sitting in the backseat. Their mom turned around. "You boys look nice," she said. "Thanks for getting ready so quackly."

Brian burst out laughing.

"What's so funny?" his mother asked.

"You said *quackly,* Mom, instead of *quickly,*" Brian said.

"Did I?" their mom said. "How strange."

Mr. Pinto glanced up at the sky. "I don't like the look of those clouds," he said. "I'll bet it rains before we get home."

"Oh, too bad," his wife said. "I wanted to sit out on the duck."

"You want to sit on the deck, hon," her husband said. "Not on the duck."

"Oh, yes, silly me," Mrs. Pinto said.

"Here we are," Mr. Pinto said a few minutes later. He parked at the end of Oak Street. The restaurant was straight ahead, near the riverbank. A wooden deck faced the water. There were tables and chairs on the deck, but no people.

"How lovely!" their mother said. "There are ducks on the river! I love watching them swim!"

Brian grinned. "Me too, Mom!" he said. "I think ducks are just wonderful!"

"Oh, brother," Bradley muttered.

The Pinto family stepped inside the restaurant. A sign just inside the door read: HAPPY MOTHER'S DAY! Bradley noticed that there were a lot of families already eating.

A man wearing a white shirt and a tie approached them. "May I seat you for lunch?" he asked.

"Yes, please," Bradley's mom said. "By the windows, please."

The man bowed. "Right this way, folks!" He took them to a booth with a view of the river. He placed five menus on the table. "Happy Mother's Day. Your server today will be Mandy."

"Oh, look," Bradley's mother said. "Aren't the ducks cute? Let's save some fries so we can feed them after lunch."

"What will you have, boys?" their father asked.

"A rare cheeseburger," Josh said. "With fries and pickles."

"Me too!" said Brian. "Only I want mine well done. Rare burgers are gross, with all that blood left on your plate."

"Well, talking about blood is even grosser," Josh said.

"Cool it, boys," their father said.

Bradley chose his favorite, macaroni and cheese.

A young woman wearing an apron walked up to their table. "Hi, I'm Mandy," she said. "Have you had a chance to look at your menus?"

"Yes, thank you," Mrs. Pinto said. "Boys, why don't you order?"

Bradley, Brian, and Josh placed their orders.

"Can we have Cokes, Mom?" Josh asked.

"No, three milks," their mother told Mandy. "And I'll have the vegetable plate and a large glass of water. In fact, bring us a pitcher of water. A large one!"

Brian kicked Bradley under the table. When Bradley looked at him,

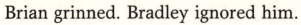

Brian grinned. Bradley ignored him.

His father ordered clam chowder and a fish dinner.

"May we go out on the deck to feed the ducks?" Brian asked when Mandy brought their food.

"After we eat," their father said. He glanced out the window. "Here comes the rain!"

They all ate. Thunder and lightning boomed and flashed.

"We're gonna get soaked when we leave," Josh said.

"So what's a little water?" their mother said. "I love getting wet in the rain. It'll be fun!"

Bradley stared at his mother. He couldn't believe his ears. Was this the same mother who never let Bradley or Brian play outside in the rain?

After lunch, the Pinto family went out onto the deck with their leftover fries. The rain had let up, and the ducks were hungry.

Bradley watched his mother feed the ducks. She was talking softly to them, too. Bradley couldn't make out the words, but they didn't sound like English. They sounded like . . . duck noises!

When the fries were gone, the family hurried toward the car. Bradley noticed a big puddle on the driveway. When they were little, he and Brian would've jumped right in and splashed each other.

"Window seat!" Josh yelled, and ran toward the car.

Brian ran after him. "Other window seat!" he called over his shoulder.

Bradley turned around to wait for his mother. His mouth fell open. She was standing in the middle of the puddle, splashing muddy water in all directions.

7
Bradley Fights Back

In the car, Bradley sat between Josh and Brian. His parents were up front, chatting away. No one else noticed that Mom's shoes were soaking wet.

Brian didn't seem to care that their mother was acting very strangely.

Josh and Dad were talking about getting night crawlers and going fishing.

Am I the only one who cares that Mom is acting like a duck? Bradley asked himself. *So what if Hypo made her look human again—she's still a duck!*

The sun was out again when they got home. Bradley went right to the phone and called Nate. "Can you come over?" he asked his friend. "It's real important! And get Lucy!"

When Bradley got to his room, Brian was on his bed, playing with an action figure. Pal was on the floor, sleeping on a pile of Brian's dirty clothes.

"I called Nate," Bradley said. "He and Lucy are coming over. We have to talk."

"About what?" Brian asked.

"About what?" Bradley repeated, not believing his ears. "Didn't you see Mom splashing in a puddle at the restaurant? And did you hear her talking to those ducks?"

"I think it's cool," Brian said, looking through his pile of comics. "And I'll bet you anything she lets me get ducks now. I might even let you help me take care of them. With all the money I make, I'll pay you a dollar an hour!"

Bradley just shook his head. He got out of his good clothes and hung them in his closet. He put on his jeans and a sweatshirt.

Just then the doorbell rang.

"Got it!" Josh yelled. Bradley could hear Josh's big feet running to open the door. "Hi, Nate. Hi, Lucy. The twins are upstairs."

A minute later Nate and Lucy walked into the room.

"What's going on?" Nate asked. "You sounded weird on the phone, Bradley."

"That's because he *is* weird," Brian said. He flopped on his bed and picked up a comic book.

"What's wrong with your mom?" Lucy asked. "She usually asks how we are, then reminds us to wipe our feet. She didn't say anything today."

"Yeah," Nate said. "She's just standing at the sink with her hands in the dishwater."

"See?" Bradley said to his brother. "They noticed, and they don't even live here!"

"Noticed what?" Nate asked.

"Ever since we got home from the high school last night, Mom's been acting strange," Bradley said. He shot his brother a look. "And Brian doesn't even care."

Brian dropped his comic. "I do too care," he said. "But I just . . . I mean I want . . ."

"Mom has been acting like a duck," Bradley said. "Since Hypo hypnotized her."

"But it was just a trick," Lucy said. "Do you really believe that white duck was your mom?"

"Guys, the duck was wearing Mom's

nail polish and her new bracelet!"
Bradley said. "Mom became a duck!"

"Anyway, Hypo hypnotized her a
second time, and she was fine," Brian
said.

"SHE'S FINE?" Bradley yelled. "Then
how do you explain why she's always

wet?" He told Nate and Lucy how Mrs. Pinto was splashing in the tub and in the puddle.

"Wow," Nate said. "That's ducky."

Bradley glared at him.

"And tell them how all this started, Brian," Bradley went on. He picked up one of Brian's comics and pointed at the ad about ducks. "Tell them about this!"

Bradley, Nate, and Lucy stared at Brian, who had turned red. "I want to get some ducks," he said. "The guy in the ad says you can collect their feathers and make money. So I asked our mom, and she said no. I'm too young, she says, and she hates ducks."

"So my brilliant brother gets Hypo to hypnotize her," Bradley added. "Suddenly my mother loves ducks. She talks to them and feeds them and plays with rubber ones in the tub! She brought corn into the bathroom!"

"What are you going to do?" Lucy asked.

"I don't know!" Bradley almost shouted. "All I know is I don't want a mom who's half duck!"

"Like Spider-Man," Nate said. "This guy got bit by a spider, and he turned into one. But only part of the time. The rest of the—"

"We all saw the movie," Bradley said. "That was make-believe. THIS IS REAL!"

The four kids were quiet. Bradley was staring out the window. Nate and Lucy were looking at each other. Brian was chewing his bottom lip. Pal was snoring.

"I know what we can do!" Lucy said. "Tell Hypo about your mom," she said. "Ask him to hypnotize her back to normal."

"But he caused the problem in the

first place!" Bradley said. "World's greatest hypnotist, my foot! I wonder how many other parents he's turned into farm animals!"

"But maybe he didn't finish the job," Nate said. "The first time he tried, he turned your mom into a duck. The second time, he turned her back into your mom, only . . ."

"Only she's still part duck!" Brian added.

"So if he does it a third time, your mom should be perfect again!" Lucy said.

Just then they heard a noise in the hallway. Bradley opened the door. Josh was walking past, shoving a cookie in his mouth.

Bradley closed the door. "How do we find Hypo?" he asked. "I'll do anything to get my real mom back."

8
Darlene to the Rescue

"Hypo could live anywhere, even California," Nate said.

"But he might be staying in Green Lawn for a while," Lucy said. "Last night he told us he grew up here."

"Wait, he said he used to work at the Shangri-la Hotel," Brian said. "So maybe he's staying there!"

"Excellent, Bri," Bradley said. "Let's go!" He woke up Pal and snapped on his leash.

The four kids hurried downstairs and through the kitchen. No one was around. Bradley heard laughter coming from the living room.

They fast-walked through the high school playing fields, toward Main Street. Pal barked at the swans as they passed the pond.

Five minutes later they entered the lobby of the hotel. Mr. Linkletter was standing behind the counter. He smiled when he saw the kids, but shook his head at Pal.

"No doggies allowed," he said. "Not even my old pal Pal."

"Hi, Mr. Linkletter. We came to see Mr. Hypo," Bradley said.

Mr. Linkletter raised his eyebrows. "Is he expecting you?" he asked.

"No, but it's really important," Nate said. "It's a matter of life and death!"

"Indeed!" Mr. Linkletter said. A smile crossed his lips, then flew away like a scared hummingbird. "I'll call his room."

Mr. Linkletter picked up the hotel phone. He tapped a number. "Mr. Grabowski, there are four children down here to see you," he said. "And a dog. They said it's a matter of life and death. . . . Yes, of course."

Mr. Linkletter hung up the phone. "Mr. Grabowski will see you," he said. "Room 207, second floor. Pal will have to stay here with me."

"Hypo's real name is Grabowski?" Nate said.

"It is indeed," Mr. Linkletter said. He walked around the counter and took Pal's leash from Bradley.

"Thanks a lot, Mr. Linkletter," Bradley said.

The four kids found the elevator and got off on the second floor. They followed the signs to room 207. The long hallway was quiet.

"This place is creepy," Brian whispered. "What if he hypnotizes us and makes us zombies or something?"

"Dude, hypnosis only works if you want it to," Nate said. "Do you want to be a zombie?"

"Let me think about it," Brian said.

Bradley knocked on the door. It was opened by a total stranger.

The man standing there was short and bald. He wore a baggy sweatshirt.

"Is Mr. Grabowski here?" Bradley asked.

"I am he!" the man said. "Better known as Hypo, the world's greatest hypnotist."

Bradley recognized Hypo's voice.

"Come in, come in," the man said.

The four kids walked in. They were in a living room with nice furniture and a big TV. Bradley saw Hypo's fake mustache on a table. Some doors led to other rooms.

"Please have a seat," Hypo said.

The kids lined up on the sofa.

Just then a big white duck waddled into the room. The duck's toenails were pink.

Bradley nearly swallowed his tongue.

Brian ran over to the duck. "Mom?" he said. "Is that you?"

Lucy just stared at the duck.

"Hi, Mrs. Pinto," Nate said.

Hypo laughed. "This isn't your mother," he said to Bradley and Brian.

"This is Darlene, the world's smartest duck."

"I don't get it," Bradley said. "Last night, you hypnotized our mom. She became a duck. This duck. That's why we're here, Mr. Grab—"

"Please, call me Arnold," the man said. "Your mother used to call me Arnie when we were in school together."

"You went to school with our mom?" Brian said.

Hypo nodded. "Yes, didn't she tell you? We graduated from high school together. I was so surprised when she called me."

"Mom called you?" Bradley asked.

"Yep. Yesterday afternoon." Hypo winked at the kids. "That was some funny trick she played on you, wasn't it?"

The four kids just stared at Hypo. All four mouths were open. Bradley felt dizzy, like the time he'd had sunstroke.

"It was . . . the duck was . . . it was all a joke?" Brian said.

"Yes, of course!" Hypo said. "Your mom told me she heard you two talking in your bedroom. Something about getting me to hypnotize her so she'd let Brian have ducks. Which one is Brian?"

"I am," Brian said. "So the whole thing was fake?"

"I'm afraid so," Hypo said. "It was your mom's idea to put her bracelet around Darlene's neck. I'm the one who thought of painting her toenails."

"The bracelet and nail polish made us think it was really Mom," Bradley said. His brain was doing flip-flops.

"Yes, your mom and I had such fun planning this together," Hypo said.

"May I hold Darlene?" Lucy asked.

Hypo settled Darlene in Lucy's arms. "Anyway, your mom asked for my help in playing the trick on you," he went on. "But you look so surprised. Didn't she tell you the whole thing was a joke? Even your dad and your brother Josh were in on it."

"That is so cool!" Nate said. "We all thought she really became a duck!"

"And she's still pretending to be one," Brian said.

"Oh, she's so naughty," Hypo said. "Pammy told me she was going to tell you the truth on the way home last night."

"Pammy must have forgotten," Bradley said. He thought of his mom splashing in the puddle. The corn on the bathroom floor. The rubber duckies in the tub. It was all a big fat joke!

Then Bradley grinned. He had an idea. "Arnold, may we borrow Darlene for an hour?" he asked.

9
The Last Laugh

Hypo looked at Bradley. "May I ask why you want to borrow my duck?" he said.

Bradley grinned and explained his plan.

"I love it!" Hypo said when Bradley had finished. "I'll even drive you home. But you have to promise that I can watch!"

Brian, Nate, and Lucy loved the idea, too. Five minutes later, they were all piled in Hypo's car with Darlene.

Pal gave Darlene a doggy kiss in the backseat. Bradley gave Hypo directions to his house.

"Park behind the barn so Mom and Dad won't see us," Brian told Hypo. "Then we can all sneak in the back door."

The four kids, Pal, and Hypo, who was carrying Darlene, tiptoed into the house. Bradley peeked into the living room. His parents and Josh were playing cards. Bradley led the others quietly up the stairs. They crept into his bedroom and closed the door.

"This is more fun than hypnotizing people!" Hypo said. "Where can I hide?"

"In my closet," Brian said. "Just kick my stuff out of the way."

But first, he pulled down the covers on his bed. Bradley grabbed Brian's I'M BRIAN T-shirt off the floor and put it on Darlene. She let out a soft quack.

"She looks so cute in it!" Lucy said.

"Yeah, much cuter than Brian when he wears it," Nate said.

Hypo settled Darlene in Brian's bed. He pulled the covers over her head. "No quacking," Hypo told Darlene.

Brian hid under his bed with Pal.

Hypo, Nate, and Lucy squeezed into the closet.

"Okay, I'll be right back," Bradley whispered. "No giggling!"

Nate giggled.

Bradley ran down the stairs. He burst into the living room. "Mom! Dad!" he cried. "Something is wrong with Brian! He's in bed making awful sounds!"

Bradley's parents dropped their cards and followed Bradley up the stairs. Josh was right behind them, chomping on a cookie.

They ran into the twins' bedroom.

"See, there he is!" Bradley said, pointing to the lump under Brian's blanket.

Bradley's mother pulled the blanket back. "Brian, what are you do—" she started to say.

But it wasn't Brian looking back at her.

It was Darlene, the duck.

Darlene looked at Mrs. Pinto.

Mrs. Pinto looked at Darlene.

Under the bed, Brian let out a loud

"QUACK, QUACK, QUACK!"

Josh burst out laughing. "They got you back, Mom!" he yelled.

Then everyone laughed. Nate, Lucy, and Hypo piled out of the closet. They were red from trying not to laugh.

The only two not laughing were Darlene and Pal.

They just looked at each other as if to say, "Humans are strange!"

If you like Calendar Mysteries, you might want to read A to Z Mysteries!

Help Dink, Josh, and Ruth Rose . . .

. . . solve mysteries from A to Z!